JUST FOR ME

NAOMI J. COLLINGTON

ISBN: 9798862764185

Cover design by: NJC
Library of Congress Control Number: 2023920236
Printed in the United States of America

DEDICATION

This book is dedicated to DeeDee, Boogie, Pebbles, Curly, Bella, Ivy, Myles, Nova, Sammie, Noel, and Remy.

"Dogs are not our whole lives, but they make our lives whole."

Roger Caras

ACKNOWLEDGMENTS

Thank you to my two beautiful children for allowing me to experience a new childhood with each of you. Thank you for inspiring me and for supporting me every step of the way. I hope I make you as proud of me and I am of the both of you.

Many thanks to my friends Vy and JD for pushing me to go ahead and put my stories onto paper for others to read. I owe this leap of faith to you.

Last but not least, while you can't read, I am thankful to my four-legged best friend, Remy. You are more than an emotional support animal. Thank you for your unconditional love.

JUST FOR ME

Before I knew you, you were just for me.

Mom and Dad said that it was just meant to be.

They saw you at the shelter, and Mom kneeled to

say hi. You snuggled close to Mom's belly, and Dad

said,

"Yep, that's the guy"!

When they brought you home, you stayed in my room-to-be.

It was as if you just couldn't wait to see me.

The magical day came when I finally arrived.

You were waiting by the door, never one to hide.

You always stayed close, as close as could be.

I guess I was just for you like you were just for me.

I got a little older and began crawling all over the
place.

You were there, always ready to play chase.

Sometimes we would play fetch or hide-and-seek.

Neither of us were any good, since we couldn't help
but peek.

Some days Mom would catch us on the floor

taking a nap.

I would never tell her, but at times I liked that

better than being on her lap.

Even when we ate, we would never separate.

You loved it when I gave you the food off my plate.

Yep, you always stayed close, as close as could be.

Because I was just for you and you just for me.

I always felt like the luckiest girl on the block.

Way better than Kasi who only had a pet rock.

You could jump, and talk, well bark, but it was

the same to me.

It was so fun watching you chase Mrs. Andrews'

mean cat up the tree.

Whenever we walked around, you were like a

protective big brother.

You never let me and strangers get close to one

another.

As a ten-year old, I thought forever we would be.

Me just for you and you just for me.

I often wondered why Mom and Dad never had
another me or you for that matter.
You always hear people talk about how they love to
hear little feet patter.
Kasi and Angie and John all had brothers and
sisters.
All I had was you and after school visitors.

Don't get me wrong, I wasn't mad; I kept it in my
head.

You were the only one I would ever let share my
bed.

It's just the more days passed; it would only be...

Me just for you and you just for me.

As I made it to high school, you were still around.

Sadly, you had gotten old and could barely hear a sound.

I was still happy to have you and cherished our time in every way.

I remember Mom and Dad buying you a cap too for graduation day.

You sat on Dad's lap, and I was excited you came.

They said everyone laughed as you barked when they called my name.

They knew you didn't hear it; you simply saw me cross the stage.

Your love for me was still as strong at your age.

That day, everyone in the stands could see.

I was just for you and you just for me.

I'm glad Mom and Dad had the conversation
with me.
They gently warned me that one day you would
no longer be.
They said that no matter what, you would be in
our hearts.
Just like the trees shed leaves, we would soon
part.

Not many get the chance to have friends for as

long as I had you.

Your heart loyal and forever true.

I held you by the door for what seemed like

forever.

Mom and Dad let me be as they got your things

together.

Our time at the vet was silent and sweet.

I put your pic on the memory tree across from

the treats.

Along with your picture for all to see, I placed a

note that said...Just for me.

I'm married now with a family of my own.

On one wall is a collage of photos of you from
being a puppy to full grown.

Mom and Dad were right; forever in our hearts
you would be.

I can't help but smile when Zoe looks at her pup
and says…

Just For Me!

ABOUT THE AUTHOR

Naomi J. Collington is a military veteran and mother of three - a daughter, son, and a pit bull. She enjoys reflecting on some of her favorite childhood memories and sharing them with others. Some of her hobbies include reading, listening to music, and traveling.

Made in the USA
Middletown, DE
15 November 2023

42801279R00015